GRANDMA
AND THE GREAT GOURD

A Bengali Folktale

Retold by CHITRA BANERJEE DIVAKARUNI

Illustrated by SUSY PILGRIM WATERS

A NEAL PORTER BOOK
ROARING BROOK PRESS
NEW YORK

Once upon a time, in a little village in India, there lived an old woman whom everyone called Grandma. She loved gardening and had the best vegetable patch in the village.

Grandma lived by herself in a little hut at the edge of the village, next to a deep, dark jungle. At times she could hear herds of elephants lumbering on forest paths, *thup-thup-thup*, or giant lizards slithering over dry leaves, *khash-khash*.

She didn't mind because she had two loyal dogs, Kalu and Bhulu, to protect her. They also helped her with garden chores.

One day, Grandma received a letter from her daughter, who lived on the other side of the jungle.

"Please come and visit me," said the letter. "I haven't seen you in so long. I miss you."

Grandma missed her daughter, too, and decided to visit her. She was a little scared about traveling through the jungle where so many fierce animals lived. But then she said, "What's life without a little adventure?"

She packed her
things and said good-bye
to her dogs. "Don't worry, boys,"
she told them. "I'll be back soon! Don't
forget to take care of my garden."
"*Gheu-gheu!*" said the dogs. "We won't forget!
We'll chase away all the wild animals, and we'll
listen for you. If you get in trouble, just call for us."

As Grandma was traveling through the jungle, *khut-khut-khut*, she came upon a clever red fox. "Ah, Grandma!" he said, baring his pointy teeth and smacking his lips. "How nice of you to arrive just when I'm so hungry!"

Grandma's heart went
dhip-dhip, but she didn't let the
fox see how scared she was.
"If you're planning to have me for
breakfast," she said, "that's a terrible idea.
See how skinny I am? I'll be a lot plumper
on my way back from my daughter's house
because she's such a good cook. You can
eat me then, if you like."
"That sounds good!" said the fox,
and he let her go.

Grandma walked deeper into the jungle, *khut-khut-khut*. In a while, she came upon a shaggy black bear.

"Ah, Grandma!" he said, flexing his claws and sharpening them on a nearby rock. "How nice of you to arrive just when I'm so hungry!"

Grandma's heart went *dhuk-dhuk*, but she didn't let the bear see how scared she was.

"If you're planning to have me for lunch," she said, "that's a terrible idea. See how thin I am? I'll be a lot fatter on my way back from my daughter's house because she's such a good cook. You can eat me then, if you like."

"That sounds good!" said the bear, and he let her go.

Grandma walked into the deepest part of the jungle, *khut-khut-khut*. Suddenly she came upon a sleek, striped tiger.

"Ah, Grandma!" he said, crouching low and swishing his tail. "How nice of you to arrive just when I'm so hungry!"

Grandma's heart went *doom-doom,* but she didn't let the tiger see how scared she was.

"If you're planning to
have me for dinner," she said
"that's a terrible idea. See how bony
I am? I'll be a lot juicier on my way back from
my daughter's house because she's such a good
cook. You can eat me then, if you like."

"That sounds good!" said the tiger, and he let her go.

Grandma reached
her daughter's house. She had
a wonderful time there, playing
with her grandchildren and telling the neighbors
all about her adventures in the forest.
She worked in her daughter's garden, watering,
digging, and sprinkling the ground with her special
fish-bone fertilizer until the vegetables grew so large
that people from three villages came to admire them.
She ate the delicious dishes her daughter cooked
and, just as she'd told the forest animals,
she grew quite plump!

But Grandma missed her dogs.

She wondered if they had guarded her garden or if they had let the mice and birds eat everything up, *kutur-kutur-kut*?

Finally, she told her daughter, "It's time for me to go home. Kalu and Bhulu are waiting for me, and so is my vegetable garden. The only problem is, the tiger, bear, and fox are waiting, too! And this time I won't be able to trick them with words."

"Don't worry!" said the daughter. "We'll come up with a plan!"

"I guess I could do that," said the bear. "I wonder when that old woman's coming back, though. I'm getting terribly hungry." He gave the gourd a powerful swipe with his paw and sent it spinning down the path.

Chat-pat, chat-pat, spun the gourd.

"*Baap re baap!*" said Grandma. "That was close!"

"It's a good thing the walls of this gourd are so thick and strong or by now I'd be dizzy as a dervish." And she ate some more puffed rice and tamarind.

The gourd rolled and bounced and spun until it was almost at the edge of the forest.

Only a little while longer! thought Grandma.

Just then the gourd reached the part of the trail where the fox was waiting for Grandma.

"What's this now?" he cried, sniffing around the gourd.

Grandma chanted, "I'm just a spinning gourd, singing my song. Won't you give me a push and help me along?"

But the clever fox said, "One hundred and one times I've sneaked into villages to steal chickens, but I've never seen a singing gourd! Something odd is going on here." He grabbed the top of the gourd with his sharp, pointy teeth and shook it back and forth until the rice glue cracked and the stitches broke off.

Out fell Grandma, *dhap-dhapash*!

"Ah, Grandma!" grinned the fox.
"How nice and plump you look!
Whatever were you doing
inside a gourd?"

"You caught me fair and square,"
said Grandma. "I guess you deserve to
eat me up. But I have a request. Can I sing
one last song before you start chewing on me?"
  "Oh, all right," said the fox, drooling a little. "Just
don't make it too long."
  "I won't!" said Grandma. At the top of her voice
she sang,
  "Kalu, Bhulu, *tu-tu-tu*!
    Kalu, Bhulu, come to me, do!
    Kalu, Bhulu, I need you!"

Back in the village, Kalu and Bhulu heard Grandma's voice. They knew she was in danger. Quick as wind, *hoosh-hoosh,* they flew into the forest, fangs bared, growling horribly. They chased the fox away, scaring him so much that he never came back.

Grandma gave her dogs a big hug.

"Thank you, boys!" she cried. "You saved my life!"

"*Gheu! Gheu!*" said Kalu and Bhulu modestly. "It was nothing!"

Once upon a time, in a little village in India, there lived an old woman whom everyone called Grandma. She loved gardening and had the best vegetable patch in the village.

Grandma lived by herself in a little hut at the edge of the village, next to a deep, dark jungle. At times she could hear herds of elephants lumbering on forest paths, *thup-thup-thup*, or giant lizards slithering over dry leaves, *khash-khash*.

She didn't mind because she had two loyal dogs, Kalu and Bhulu, to protect her. They also helped her with garden chores.

One day, Grandma received a letter
from her daughter, who lived on the other
side of the jungle.

"Please come and visit me," said the letter.
"I haven't seen you in so long. I miss you."

Grandma missed her daughter, too, and
decided to visit her. She was a little scared about
traveling through the jungle where so many fierce
animals lived. But then she said, "What's life without
a little adventure?"